Not I, Not I

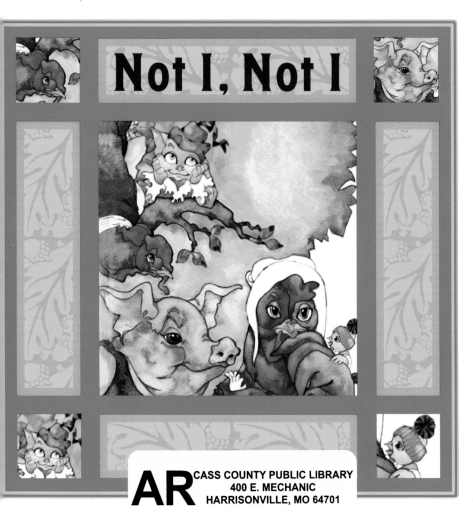

by Margaret Hillert

Illustrated by Diana Magnuson

NORWOOD HOUSE 🏠 PRESS

DEAR CAREGIVER, The *Beginning-to-Read* series is a carefully written collection of classic readers you may remember from your own childhood. Each book features text comprised of common sight words to provide your child ample practice reading the words that appear most frequently in written text. The many additional details in the pictures enhance the story and offer the opportunity for you to help your child expand oral language and develop comprehension.

Begin by reading the story to your child, followed by letting him or her read familiar words and soon your child will be able to read the story independently. At each step of the way, be sure to praise your reader's efforts to build his or her confidence as an independent reader. Discuss the pictures and encourage your child to make connections between the story and his or her own life. At the end of the story, you will find reading activities and a word list that will help your child practice and strengthen beginning reading skills.

Above all, the most important part of the reading experience is to have fun and enjoy it!

Shannon Cannon

Shannon Cannon,
Literacy Consultant

Norwood House Press • P.O. Box 316598 • Chicago, Illinois 60631
For more information about Norwood House Press please visit our website at
www.norwoodhousepress.com or call 866-565-2900.

LIBRARY OF CONGRESS CATALOGING-IN-PUBLICATION DATA

Hillert, Margaret.
  Not I, not I : The little red hen retold / Margaret Hillert; illustrated
by Diana Magnuson. — Rev. and expanded library ed.
  p. cm. — (Beginning-to-read book)
  Summary: The little red hen finds none of her friends willing to help with her crop
but all are eager to eat the bread she makes from it. Includes reading activities.
  ISBN-13: 978-1-59953-052-9 (library binding : alk. paper)
  ISBN-10: 1-59953-052-X (library binding : alk. paper)
  [1. Folklore.] I. Magnuson, Diana, ill. II. Little red hen. III. Title.
  IV. Series: Hillert, Margaret. Beginning to read series. Fairy tales and folklore.
  PZ8.1.H539No 2007
  398.2—dc22
  [E]   2006007897

Beginning-to-Read series (c) 2007 by Margaret Hillert.
Library edition published by permission of Pearson Education, Inc. in
arrangement with Norwood House Press, Inc. All rights reserved.
This book was originally published by Follett Publishing Company in 1981.
Manufactured in the United States of America in North Mankato, Minnesota.
180R-042011

Here is a mother.
The mother is little.
The mother is red.

Look here.
Here is a little baby.
The baby is yellow.
It can run and play.

See the yellow baby run.
See it run to Mother.
It said, "Mother, Mother.
I want something."

Mother said, "Come and look.
Help me find something.
Away we go."

Look, look.
Here is something.
Something little.
I can work.
I can make it big.

Oh, oh.
Look here.
One, two, three.
Can you help me?

Not I.
Not I.
Not I.
We can not help.

I can.
I can work.
See it go down here.

Look, look.
See where it is.
It is up.
It is big, big, big.

Can you help?
Can you three help me?
Come and work.

Not I.
Not I.
Not I.
We can not help.

17

It is funny.
You can not work.
You can not help.
I can work.

Here I go.
Away, away.
Can you come?
Can you help?

19

Not I.
Not I.
Not I.
We can not help.

See, see.
It is in here.
I can make something.

I can work.
See me work.
I can make something.

Look here, baby.
It can go in here.
It is for you.

Here it is.
Come and look.
Oh, oh.
Can you help me?

I can.
I can.
I can.
We can help.

Oh, oh.
We see it.
We want it.

Not you.
Not you.
Not you.
Go away.
It is for my little baby and me.

The following activities support the findings of the National Reading Panel that determined the most effective components for reading instruction are: Phonemic Awareness, Phonics, Vocabulary, Fluency, and Text Comprehension.

Phonemic Awareness: The long i sound

Oddity Task: Say the long **i** sound (as in I or ice) for your child. Ask your child to say the word that has the long **i** sound in the following word groups:

bike, bin, bid	whiff, wife, win	in, fin, ice
sit, sip, side	pin, pen, pine	light, lit, let
red, rid, ride	chimp, champ, child	

Phonics: The letter Ii

1. Demonstrate how to form the letters **I** and **i** for your child.
2. Have your child practice writing **I** and **i** at least three times each.
3. Ask your child to point to the words in the book that begin with the letter **i**.
4. Write the words listed below on separate pieces of paper. Read each word aloud and ask your child to repeat them.

tie	rice	try	pie	sky	sigh
five	like	light	kind	nice	shy
high	fly	climb	night	ice	slide

5. Write the following long **i** spellings at the top of a piece of paper

    i   i_e   ie   igh

6. Ask your child to sort the words by placing them under the correct long **i** spelling.

Vocabulary: Personal Pronouns

1. Explain to your child that words that can be substituted for the names of people are called pronouns.

2. Write the following words on separate pieces of paper:

    I   me   he   she   we   you   they
3. Read each word to your child and ask your child to repeat it.

4. Mix the words up. Point to a word and ask your child to read it. Provide clues if your child needs them.

5. Read the following sentences to your child. Ask your child to provide an appropriate pronoun to complete the sentence.

    • The mother in the story is red. ____is also little.

    • She asked the others, "Can ____ help me?"

    • The mother told the others to go away. She said, "Go away. It is for my baby and ____."

    • The others did not help. ____ did not work.

    • When the mother put the food out, the others said, "____ can help."

Fluency: Echo Reading

1. Reread the story to your child at least two more times while your child tracks the print by running a finger under the words as they are read. Ask your child to read the words he or she knows with you.

2. Reread the story, stopping after each sentence or page to allow your child to read (echo) what you have read. Repeat echo reading and let your child take the lead.

Text Comprehension: Discussion Time

1. Ask your child to retell the sequence of events in the story.

2. To check comprehension, ask your child the following questions:

    • What is the mother getting on page 7?

    • Why didn't the three others want to help the mother?

    • Why did the others say they could help at the end of the story?

    • Why is the baby the only one who got to eat?

    • What is the lesson in this story?

WORD LIST

Not I, Not I uses the 44 words listed below.

This list can be used to practice reading the words that appear in the text. You may wish to write the words on index cards and use them to help your child build automatic word recognition. Regular practice with these words will enhance your child's fluency in reading connected text.

a	help	oh	up
and	here	one	
away			want
	I	play	we
baby	in		where
big	is	red	work
	it	run	
can			yellow
come	little	said	you
	look	see	
down		something	
	make		
find	me	the	
for	mother	three	
funny	my	to	
		two	
go	not		

ABOUT THE AUTHOR Margaret Hillert has written over 80 books for children who are just learning to read. Her books have been translated into many different languages and over a million children throughout the world have read her books. She first started writing poetry as a child and has continued to write for children and adults throughout her life. A first grade teacher for 34 years, Margaret is now retired from teaching and lives in Michigan where she likes to write, take walks in the morning, and care for her three cats.

Photograph by G...

ABOUT THE ADVISER Shannon Cannon contributed the activities pages that appear in this book. Shannon serves as a literacy consultant and provides staff development to help improve reading instruction. She is a frequent presenter at educational conferences and workshops. Prior to this she worked as an elementary school teacher and as president of a curriculum publishing company.